# Diary of a Horse Mad Girl

## Book 2

## *Pony Club Adventures*

### By Katrina Kahler

Copyright © KC Global Enterprises

## Dedication

This story is dedicated to Linda, Glen and Alyce. Without their ongoing, friendship, support and generosity, many of the adventures in this series would never have happened.

*Shelley…at pony club*

## Wednesday 2 January

Last night was the scariest night of my life!!! I overheard Mom and Dad talking. They were saying that if the rain keeps up, the creek is definitely going to flood. I knew that if it did, Sparkle wouldn't be able to cross over to the big paddock to be near the other horses. If she wasn't near them during the storm, she'd be really scared. And if she got spooked in the storm, then she could be seriously hurt.

Mom and Dad were in the kitchen cooking dinner and Nate was watching TV. So I decided to sneak out the front door. I went downstairs, got my gumboots and a raincoat and grabbed Sparkle's halter and lead rope. I just had to go and find her!

It was absolutely pouring with rain and by that time, it was really dark. I wasn't scared at all though because all I could think of was my baby.

Mom and Dad have commented before on how brave I am. Our car was stuck up near the front gate once, because a huge tree had fallen across the drive in some gale force winds. And the next night, I walked all the way up there on my own in the pitch black darkness so I could get something out of the car. I can't even remember what it was now. But it didn't bother me at all. My brother Nate would never do that! He's even too scared to go downstairs at night on his own. He's such a chicken!

Luckily I had a torch with me when I went to look for Sparkle tonight though. Otherwise, I don't think I would've been able to find her. She was standing under a tree and I heard her whinny when she saw me. I know she was glad that I was there.

I got the halter and lead rope on her and led her down to the creek to the spot where we usually cross. There was so much rain, I couldn't see that well, even with Dad's big torch. But then all of a sudden my gumboots filled up with water. The creek was definitely getting higher and I had to go really slowly across the rocks. Sparkle was walking along with me – lucky she's such a bomb proof horse otherwise I don't think I would've been able to get her to cross.

Just as we were about half way, I felt the lead rope pull really hard! I looked back to see what had happened and realized Sparkle had slipped into the deeper part of the creek! My heart was thumping so hard, I could feel it pounding against my chest. But all I could think about was saving her. I was standing on the trail of rocks where we always cross and I could feel the water really pulling me – it was so strong! I had to grip so hard to keep myself from being washed in.

I called out – Sparkle! Sparkle! – She was neighing and neighing but all I could do was pull on the lead rope. I was so scared! Then all of a sudden she managed to scramble back up onto the rocks. I have no idea how she did that – but I'm so glad she did! I was so desperate to get her across the creek that I just kept on going. I knew that she trusted me and would follow me anywhere!

We kept going and finally made it to the other side. Then we had to climb the hill. It was really muddy and slippery and we kept sliding down - it was so hard to make our way up. I fell over but she kept going and that helped to pull me to my feet. I'm glad I was able to get up otherwise she would've dragged me through the mud. We got to the top and I took off her halter and lead rope then let her go. Straight away, she raced into the paddock looking for the other horses. I knew once she found them, she'd be ok.

Then I had to get back down the hill. I had to hang onto tree branches so I didn't go sliding down into the creek. I knew that I was totally covered in mud, but I didn't care. The creek was rising and I just wanted to get back home. It was such a struggle to keep my boots on and push against the force of all the rushing water.

I felt so glad when I finally made it to the other side! I rushed back across the grass and one of my boots came off as I was running. So I had to go back and find it. When I made it back to the house, I left my muddy boots and raincoat downstairs. Then I sneaked back in the front door and into my room to get changed. Just then, I could hear Mom calling me for dinner.

When she saw me, she said she'd been wandering around the house looking for me. She asked why my hair was all wet. Then I started to cry. I just couldn't help it! When she asked me what was wrong, I had to tell her. And she just stood there staring at me. She thought I'd been in my room the whole time.

Mom and Dad both said they were in shock thinking about what could have happened. They said that Sparkle could have dragged me into the creek or fallen on top of me or anything. They said that I could have been washed away and drowned! They said that they wouldn't have known where to look for me because they had no idea I'd even left the house.

Now I'm worried that Sparkle might have hurt her back when she slipped over.

I can't stop writing tonight. So much has happened and I just have to write about it all. Mom says that writing things down really helps when you're upset.

It all feels like a really bad dream – I can't believe it happened. Just last night, I was having so much fun with my friends and tonight Sparkle and I could have drowned. I think that Mom and Dad are still in shock as well! At least they didn't get angry at me. I think they understand how I was feeling. And I think they're just glad that I'm safe!

## Thursday 3 January

Thank goodness Sparkle is okay! We drove around to Ali's house today to check on her. With the creek flooded, it's the only way we can get to her paddock. I heard her nicker as soon as she saw me. She trotted straight over to where I was standing and nuzzled up to me. I think she knows that I saved her last night and now we're even closer than ever. I love her and she loves me. She's my best friend in the whole world!

*Our whole grass area was flooded!* ☹

## Sunday 6 January

It's been really hectic this week. It's still pouring with rain and the creek is still way too high to cross. There's been flooding everywhere and some poor people have even had their houses go under water.

Nate's happy though because the cyclone up north is making the surf really big. And Dad's been taking him and his friend surfing nearly every day this week. Those huge waves look so scary, but Nate loves it! I can't work out why he's so scared of horse riding. Surfing and motorbike riding seem so much scarier to me! Dad's tried to teach me how to surf a couple of times, but I couldn't stand up. We took Grace with us to the beach one time and she stood up straight away. Dad said she has really good balance. I got annoyed because I couldn't do it and she could. I don't like surfing anyway. I'd much rather ride horses!!!

Anyway, Mom or Dad has to drive me around to Ali's every morning and afternoon to check on the horses and feed them. I wish our paddocks weren't across the creek! The paddocks are so muddy and sloshy and our poor babies have to just stand in the rain. Lucky there's the big tree in the paddock for them to shelter under and at least they all have rugs on to help protect them.

Millie now has mud fever though! That's because she's standing in mud all day. Shelley had to call the vet and he said that so many horses have this problem at the moment. It's because of all the rain. Her legs have got this terrible infection all over them, especially around her feet. Now, I have to put some special betadine spray on them twice a day to help it all heal. She has medicine to take as well and I have to mix it in her feed. Shelley comes to look after her when she can, but she lives too far away to come every day.

I'm so lucky that Sparkle has such good feet. Everyone says that about her. She doesn't even need horse shoes! That saves us a lot of money because we only have to get her hooves trimmed occasionally, rather than paying for new shoes all the time.

When's this rain going to stop? The weather man said it's not supposed to clear up for another few days yet. Nate's keen for the creek to go down so he can have some fun playing in there. When there's plenty of fresh rain water, he paddles around on our big surf ski. And last summer he even caught a turtle. But I just want to go riding. I miss hanging out in the paddock with all the girls and spending time with my baby. It's the school holidays and we're all stuck indoors. At least the Saddle Club is on TV twice a day during the holidays. I get to watch it in the morning AND in the afternoon. It's the best show ever!

*Me on our rope swing last summer* ☺

## Thursday 10 January

FINALLY the rain stopped enough today for us to tack up and have a little ride. The paddocks are so wet though and the only place we could ride was up and down Ali's driveway. I had to give all my tack and my boots a good clean last night. They were covered in mold from all the wet weather - it was disgusting!

When Tom came down to check on Cammie and Grace's horses this afternoon, he told us that he's found a great place for us to ride. It's in the state forest and he said there's lots of great trails. Also, it's only about one mile from here and we can easily ride there and then back home again afterwards.

So next week, Tom is going to take us and show us the way. We need an adult to go with us, just to be safe. He doesn't have a horse of his own to ride but Ali's mom said that he can ride her horse, Bugsy. Her horse is called that because he always gets attacked by bugs - especially mosquitoes. She has to keep him rugged all the time when he's not being ridden. She also has to put this special stuff on him to keep the bugs away. It's like an animal insect repellent. I think I should use some on Sparkle as well because I've noticed some bites on her lately too. Ali's mom doesn't ride much and she likes to see Bugsy being exercised. She said that a long ride like that will be good for him.

My first ever real trail ride on Sparkle and all of us are going together.

This will be really cool.

I can't wait!

## Wednesday 16 January

Today was awesome! We all met in the paddock at 6am. We had to be tacked up and ready because Tom wanted to get going as early as possible before it got hot. We all followed him down the driveway, out the gate and down our street. I was so excited! Then when we got to the main road, we all had to dismount and lead our horses because it's too dangerous to ride them along there. This part was really scary! There's not really a proper footpath on the side of the road to walk on, so we had to be really careful. It was especially scary when semi-trailers went past. It seemed like they were only about 3 feet away from us and we could feel the wind as they drove along. They seemed to be going so fast. Even though I was scared, I still felt safe though, because Sparkle is so bomb proof - nothing seems to spook her. Also, because we were with Tom.

It was quite a long way to get to the entrance of the state forest but when we headed off the main road, we could ride again. Sparkle got so excited. All the other horses were walking but she just wanted to trot. So I had to go in the lead. And she's got such a quick trot! Everyone comments on her trot, but I'm used to it.

When we got into the forest, we had to ride single file. Ali was in the lead, I was in the middle and Tom was at the back. This was so he could keep an eye on everyone. And it was heaps of fun!!! There were heaps of little logs on the track and we got to jump over them. It was so fun going over all those jumps. When we were about half way, we stopped to give the horses a rest and have a snack. I gave Sparkle my banana. She loved it!

When we were riding, Tom kept saying - how's it going down there? I was on the smallest pony of all of us and he was on the biggest. He was so much bigger than me. That must have looked really funny.

Then at the end of the trail, we had to walk back along the side of the road. It wasn't as scary this time. I think the horses were glad when we finally got home though. They were all pretty tired by the end of it. That's the longest ride I've ever been on and my legs were pretty sore too - and my bottom! They're even still sore now.

We can't wait to do it again. Tom said that we might even be able to go once a week. I think he enjoyed it as much as us. He grew up on a horsey property and always had his own pony when he was a kid. He's so happy that Cammie and Grace are riding now.

I want to have my own horsey property when I grow up and I'm going to teach my children how to ride. I think I'll always have horses. I can't imagine not riding!

*I'm going to have lovely fenced paddocks like this when I grow up!*

## Sunday 20 January

Charlie's been bitten by a snake!!!!!!!!!!!!!!!!!

I can't believe it! POOR ALI! She loves that horse so much! This is terrible!

When I went to feed Sparkle this morning, I saw Ali and her mom with a beach umbrella set up in Charlie's paddock. I thought…what's going on? So I went over to check and he was lying down on the ground.

Ali said she found bite marks and blood on his leg and they called the vet. He said it was definitely a snake and had to give Charlie a needle with anti-venom. He told them to leave Charlie where he was and watch him carefully. The vet came back this afternoon but he said that there was no change. He doesn't know if Charlie's going to live!

I think Ali will probably sleep with him in the paddock tonight. I know that I would, if it happened to Sparkle. I hope he's okay. POOR ALI!!!! AND POOR CHARLIE!!!!! I feel sorry for them. It's terrible seeing him just lying there.

I don't want him to die!

## Monday 21 January

Charlie's been lying down in the same spot ALL day. The vet came 3 times to check on him. He said that Charlie seems to be improving but he won't stand up. He said that if he lives through tonight that he'll probably be ok.

I don't normally say prayers but I'm going to pray for Charlie tonight.

Please let him be okay!!!!!!!

## Tuesday 22 January

He's still lying down and he still hasn't moved from that same spot! Ali's been with him nearly the whole time. They were up all through the night checking on him.

I can't believe it's been another whole day.

PLEASE LET HIM LIVE!!!!

**Wednesday 23 January**

Charlie had to be put down today.

He finally tried to stand up this morning but then he just collapsed. The vet said that it's because he's been lying down for 3 whole days. His muscles must have become really weak and the vet said that they just pulled away from the bone. He said that he would never be able to walk.

It's so sad.

Ali is really upset. We were all crying. I'm crying right now. This is the saddest day ever!

I think they're going to bury him in the paddock. What's Ali going to do without him?

## Monday 4 February

I haven't wanted to write in my diary lately - I've been too sad about Charlie. They did bury him in the paddock and Ali's mom said they're going to plant a special tree right over his grave. That way, they'll be able to remember him forever. Not that Ali will ever forget him.

I'm back at school now. I have Miss Johnson again but that's good because she's so nice and she's a really great teacher. The whole class has stayed together and we're all so happy about that because we're all friends.

Ali said her mom has started looking for another horse for her. I hope she gets one soon. It's not the same when she's not riding with us. But Ali said she doesn't want another horse.

Tom's going to take us for another trail ride on Saturday. He's going to ride Ali's mom's horse again. Ali said that she doesn't want to go.

**Saturday 9 February**

We went for a trail ride this morning. Mom said that it was good for me to do something fun. I've been really sad since Charlie died and the trail ride helped to take my mind off him. The best news is that Ali is getting a new horse! His name is Bailey and her mom said that he's a beautiful 15 hand chestnut. He belongs to a friend of hers who doesn't have time to look after him. So she asked if Ali would like to take him. Ali didn't want to at first, because she's still so upset about Charlie. But her mom thought it would be the best thing if she were busy with another horse. So Ali agreed. I'm so glad. I'm sure it will help to cheer her up again – I hope so anyway.

I do have some really exciting news though. Pony Club sign on is next weekend! And Mom and Dad said I can go. I'm really looking forward to that!

## Sunday 17 February

We went to Pony Club sign on today. Tom was there and he introduced us to the lady who runs it. She's so nice! She has 2 daughters of her own who ride as well. No one had their horses there or anything, but Mom and Dad had to sign some forms and pay the fees. Then we bought my uniform. On pony club days, we have to wear a maroon polo shirt with our pony club emblem on it. And any jodhpurs we want. But when we're competing at gymkhanas or other competitions, we have to wear cream joddies and a special woolen vest. It's a really nice dark maroon, because that's our pony club color. I was lucky because they had some 2nd hand uniforms and I was able to get a shirt and a tie. I also had to get a special maroon saddle cloth – that's the uniform that the horses have to have so people can tell what pony club they're from.

Pony club is on every second Sunday and the first day for the year is next Sunday.

I CAN'T WAIT!!!

## Sunday 24 February

Pony Club is AWESOME!!!

Tom came over early this morning with Shelley and Kate to load their horses onto his float. He showed Dad how to hook it up properly and Dad followed him in his car. When they got to pony club and unloaded the horses, Dad brought the float back to our house. It's lucky we only live about 15 minutes away so it didn't take too long. I was standing in the driveway with Sparkle on a lead rope and all my tack, ready to get going. I just couldn't wait to get there!

I walked Sparkle onto the float with Mom and Dad helping me – luckily she went on first go and didn't even hesitate. Tom said that some people have trouble getting their horses on floats, but we watched him load Millie and Lulu. And he gave us some tips as well, so we kind of knew what to do.

When we got there, we unloaded Sparkle and tied her up to the fence with some bailing twine. Shelley and Kate saved me a spot next to them which was so cool. They said that's their spot, where they always tie up – and now it's my spot too!

They were so excited that I was there and couldn't wait to show me around and introduce me to everyone. I felt so proud wearing my new pony club shirt and being friends with Shelley and Kate. They were so nice to me and were helping me with everything. All the other girls seemed really nice too and it was just so exciting to be there with my own pony! There's a few boys who go, but not many.

First of all, we had to all line up in the arena and the instructors came around to check that we were tacked up properly and that our girths were tight enough. Then we were put into groups depending on how good a rider we are. I was with some other girls my age. I was so glad I didn't have to go with the beginners.

We were there for the whole day and rotated around all the activities. We practiced so many different things and I can tell that my riding has improved already. I loved it when we did the jumping and the instructors were so helpful. I only did small jumps but it was really fun!

The best part was when we did sporting events in the afternoon. They were timing us and Sparkle came second in the barrel racing. I was really happy! We practiced bounce pony and bending as well and she almost won those too. The instructors said that she's a great sporting pony!

Then at the end of the day, Shelly and Kate loaded their horses onto the float and Tom took them home. We just had to wait for him to bring the float back for us. He lives really close by, so he doesn't mind. I'm so lucky that he's letting us use his float or I wouldn't be able to do pony club at all. Ali, Cammie and Grace all want to go as well. But they don't have a float so they can't. I'm so lucky!

When we tried to load Sparkle this time though, she just wouldn't go on. Maybe she was tired and suddenly decided to be naughty? We kept trying and trying but she just refused. I didn't know horses could be so stubborn!

Luckily one of the instructors came and helped us. He showed us how to use a rope with 2 people holding each end and sort of wrapping it around the back of her while I led her on with the lead rope. Anyway, it worked and she went straight on. Everyone at pony club is really nice and helpful.

Just as we were leaving though, we got the fright of our lives – or Mom and Dad did anyway! When we were about to drive out onto the main road, we went over a speed bump and all of a sudden, there was a loud thumping noise. It was so lucky that Dad decided to get out and check because the horse float had come unhooked from the tow bar on our car. All that was keeping it attached was the metal chain.

Dad was able to get it hooked up properly so that it was all secure but it was so lucky that it came unstuck right there! If we'd driven out onto the main road, we would have had to go up a really big hill. And Dad said that the float would definitely have come off the car. If this happened, the float would have rolled down the hill into the cars behind us. Imagine that!!! My poor baby could have been killed and even the people in the cars as well.

That would have been a disaster! We were so lucky! Mom is still talking about what could have happened and how lucky we were! Dad's going to have to be so careful in future. He has to make sure the float is hooked up properly.

Mom and Dad don't want me to tell the girls. If Tom finds out, he mightn't lend us the float anymore.

But I don't want to think about that!

Pony club is THE BEST and I had THE BEST DAY EVER!!!!

I can't wait till we go again in 2 weeks' time.

I'm going to ride Sparkle every afternoon now and practice and practice. This will help to build up her muscle tone as well. She's going to look so good! I love going to Pony Club! It's cool!!!

## Saturday 2 March

I've been riding every afternoon this week. I've been going later when it's really shady and not so hot. Mom's been helping me with all the sporting events. She's been using my watch to time me and I'm getting quicker every day, especially with bending and bounce pony. I've been going over bigger jumps too and now I can jump 27 inches!!! That's getting so much higher. Sparkle does seem to be getting stubborn though. Sometimes she just stops at the jumps and yesterday I nearly fell off. Ali told me that she's getting used to me and wants to be the boss. So now I have to really use my leg aids and push her on. I have to be really strong and push her over the jumps. I have to show her I'm the boss!

Tomorrow the girls and I are going to go for a big ride up on our neighbor's property. They have this massive hill and heaps of land and they told Dad that it's okay for us to ride up there. We just have to watch out for their cows. And of course, be sure to shut the gate so they don't get out. It's so pretty up there.

## Sunday 3 March

Today we went through the gate onto our neighbor's big hill and the view from the top was AMAZING!!! We could see for miles and miles and there are beautiful green hills everywhere – it's so nice for riding! And we could see the Andalusian horse property just down the hill. So we decided to canter down and have a look. It was so much fun and the Andalusians are so pretty.

But then, we came across all the cows. And they had little calves with them. They were so cute. We wanted to get closer and have a look but Millie was petrified. She's such a big horse - but she's such a huge scaredy cat! She's scared of EVERYTHING!!! Even crossing our creek when there's hardly any water in it. She will not cross over it! She has to jump across. And that's a huge leap! It's scary watching her.

Anyway, when Millie got scared of all the cows today, Shelly had trouble keeping her calm. And then all of a sudden, some bulls appeared out of nowhere. This one bull just came for us! I was so scared because it started chasing us and we had to gallop down the hill to get away. And the hill was so steep – it was scary getting down. I was petrified!

Shelley told me later that it was the scariest moment of her life. She thought when the bull was chasing us, we'd get pinned to the fence. It was SO SCARY!!!

We couldn't get back into our paddock quickly enough! My heart is still thumping just thinking about it.

## Monday 4 March

When we got home from school this afternoon, there was a cow in our driveway. We couldn't work out where it had come from. But then when we got down to our house, we found there were cows everywhere. They were all over the grass – there must have been at least 20 of them!

Dad thought we must have left the gate open yesterday afternoon and that's how they got in. But I knew that we'd definitely shut it properly. We didn't want to risk that bull coming in our paddock after us, that's for sure!

But when I went over the creek to the horse paddock to check, there were no cows in there at all – thank goodness – or Millie would have gone crazy. Dad said they must have got in through the fence somewhere down near the house. But the problem was he couldn't get hold of Matt, our neighbor, to help him chase them out again. We all tried, but they just ran around on our grass and then pretty much ignored us. I think they love our grass. It really is the best grass – that's why I bring Sparkle down to graze. I hope they don't eat it all!

I shone a torch down over the balcony tonight and I could see a pair of huge eyes shining up at me. There was a cow laying down right by the house. Dad's just worried they'll destroy our garden. At least we couldn't see any bulls.

Our dog Sheba keeps barking at them. And I think that Soxy is too scared to go out at all. At least that'll stop him from trying to hunt wildlife! He's the cutest most adorable cat you've ever seen, but he's been so naughty at night time lately. Mom said that we're going to have to lock him in after dark from now on.

I can hear those cows mooing. I hope they don't keep us awake!

## Tuesday 5 March

Well, we woke up this morning, hoping the cows would be gone but they were still there. They started mooing at sunrise. We weren't happy!

At least Dad managed to get hold of Matt this afternoon and he came over and helped Dad chase them out, back over to his property. He said he found where they managed to get in and was going to mend that part of the fence.

I hope they don't get in again. Our lawn is wrecked now! It was still soft from all the rain we've had lately and now there's big potholes everywhere from their hooves. There's huge cow paddies everywhere too. I hope Dad doesn't expect me to clean all that up! I have enough horse manure to pick up as it is!

## Sunday 10 March

Pony Club again today! It was fun! Dad dropped us there and then took Nate surfing. Sheba went with them. She loves going to the beach. She spends all day trying to catch fish. Mom stayed with me at pony club – because a parent always has to stay – and plus Mom loves watching me ride. Then Dad, Nate and Sheba came back for us this afternoon.

The girls are all nice and I've made a new friend called Kelly. She's a bit older than me but she's so friendly. I love it when we stop for a lunch break and everyone just hangs out together near the clubhouse. And they make the best food. Today, they cooked burgers for everyone and they were so delicious. Everyone is always so hungry and all the food gets eaten, which is good. This helps to raise money for the pony club so they can buy new equipment and pay for some really good instructors to come and teach us.

We had a big meeting as well and they told us that our pony club gymkhana will be on Sunday 12 May. That's less than 2 months away. And that'll be my very first gymkhana! I'm so excited! I can't wait!!!!

I'm going to practice on Sparkle as much as I can – this will be cool!!!

## Saturday 16 March

So much happened today!

First of all, Dad rang Jim to find out when he's going to put Cammie and Grace's horses in our front paddock. It's been so long now since Dad bought everything for the fencing and Jim even spent a day helping to put it all up. But then today, he told Dad that he's going to keep their horses at Ali's. Dad wasn't happy because it cost him a lot of money and he only put the fence up to help Jim out. And I wasn't happy, because I was looking forward to the girls keeping their horses at my place.

Then Tom arrived with their float to pick up Kate's horse Lulu. He said that he's found a great horse property to keep her on and has decided to move her. This was more terrible news, because I didn't want Kate or Lulu to go anywhere else. And I was worried that Shelley might move as well. Then I'd be left with no one.

On top of that, I was really worried because I didn't know what would happen with Tom's float. Would I still be able to use it? Without his float, I can't get to pony club and Mom and Dad have already bought all my uniforms.

But luckily, Tom is kind and generous. He said that we can still borrow it. All we have to do is drive to his house to pick it up on pony club days. I was very glad! It would have been terrible otherwise. So now, Shelley and I will take our horses together – this will be heaps of fun!

Then just when I thought everything was going to be okay….Ali's mom and my Dad nearly started a huge bushfire!!!

Ali's mom has told us that we should burn off our small paddock – she's done this before and it can help get rid of any bad grass and weeds that are growing. Our property used to be used for cattle and our paddocks are full of a type of grass called setaria. This is good for cows but not horses. If they eat the white husks off the top, they can end up with a disease called "big head." This makes their heads get all swollen and makes them really sick. So we have to slash the grass with a big tractor type mower to keep the setaria really short and get rid of the white husks. Anyway, she suggested that burning off would really help and said that she would show us the best way to do it.

So she poured petrol in rows down the paddock and Dad set it alight. Before we knew it, there were rows of fire across our small paddock. But then all of a sudden the wind came up. It started blowing flames everywhere and I got really scared. Mom and Dad said that they were really worried as well. We were just about to call the fire brigade, but somehow, Dad managed to get it all under control.

What a day! Now we have a burnt paddock and one less horse because Lulu is gone. And as well as that, we have brand new fencing around our front paddock but no horses to keep in it.

But at least, we can still use Tom's float and we can still get to pony club. It would be terrible if we couldn't do that!

*I don't want Lulu to go!!* ☹

## Wednesday 20 March

Dad was at the hardware and stock feeds store in town today and saw an ad on the noticeboard. Someone is looking for a place to agist their 2 horses and he took their phone number so he could call them.

Anyway, it turns out that it's a lady who has a horse and also a little Welsh Mountain pony. The pony belongs to her daughter who's the same age as me. Well, she's just turned 10 and I'll be 10 at the end of the year, so it's close enough!

Dad said that they're coming over tomorrow afternoon to meet us and have a look. If it works out, he's planning for them to keep their horses in our front paddock. That way, the paddock will get used after all.

I'm excited because it's someone else who's around my age. And I haven't been seeing any of the girls much lately. So it would be so nice to have someone else to ride with.

I wonder what she's like and what their horses are like? Dad didn't really ask, so now I have to wait until I get home from school tomorrow. I searched for some photos of Welsh Mountain ponies because I didn't know what they look like. They're very cute. I wonder what hers is like? I can't wait to meet them!

## Thursday 21 March

The girl's name is Nikita and her mum's name is Jo. Jo has a 15 hand grey called Billie and Nikita has a Welsh Mountain pony called Cappy. He's only 10 hands high so he must be really small. The only worry is that because he's so little, he might actually escape by going under the fence.

Anyway, they're keen to keep them here and they're going to bring them over on Sunday. Nikita seemed very shy, but nice and Dad talked to Jo about us two girls riding together.

At least I won't have the smallest pony anymore! Yayyyy!

## Saturday 23 March

Cappy is the cutest pony I've ever seen! All the girls came over to have a look at him this afternoon after Jo and Nikita left. They all think he's cute as well. I'm really glad that they're keeping their horses here. The front paddock seems perfect for them. We think that Cappy should be okay but we'll have to keep the front gate shut just in case he does manage to escape.

I just love his shaggy mane and forelock – it's very long, it even partly covers his eyes. But he is the cutest thing ever. Nikita said that his coat gets really thick and shaggy in winter as well. We all think he's just adorable!

Dad talked to Jo again about us girls going riding together. I was too shy to ask Nikita and she's shy as well, but hopefully we can. She's really pretty and she seems really nice. Maybe I'll see her tomorrow afternoon when we get back from pony club.

I have to clean all my tack now because the instructors give us points for having clean tack. Dad said at least that will make me look after everything. I'm going to put on a Saddle Club DVD and clean it all while I'm watching the show. I'm up to a really good episode – I can't wait to see what happens.

## Sunday 24 March

I couldn't go to pony club today!!! It was the worst thing ever!! Sparkle would NOT go on the float! Shelley couldn't go because she was sick, so it was just me taking Sparkle. Dad drove all the way to Tom's house to get the float, but we couldn't get her to walk on. We tried everything! Even using the rope trick didn't help. She was really stubborn, she just refused!

I was really disappointed. I've been so looking forward to it. And I even cleaned all my tack and everything last night! After about an hour of trying, I just had to take her back to the paddock. There was nothing else we could do because we had no one to help us. By that time though, I didn't want to ride and there was no one to ride with anyway. I was so keen to practice all the events for the gymkhana today too. I really need to work on my rider class and they were going to have a special instructor there today as well.

I'm just going to have to practice in the paddock every afternoon. Even if it's on my own. I really need to get Sparkle ready for the gymkhana. It's only about 6 weeks away and it'll be here before I know it. But now we have to work out how to get her on the float. When Dad took it back to Tom this morning, he said it usually helps if another horse gets on, then the 2nd one will follow. So maybe if Shelley and I go together, she can put Millie on first. But then, I heard Shelley complaining the other day that she's even having trouble getting Millie on the float. So I don't know what we're going to do.

At least I saw Nikita this afternoon when she came with her mom to feed their horses. We arranged to have a ride together next weekend, so that will be fun. I'll be able to take her over to the big paddock so we can ride there. She hasn't seen Sparkle yet. I can't wait to show her off.

33

## Saturday 30 March

Nikita and her mum, Jo came over today. They were hoping to go riding in the big paddock but it's been raining all week and it's way too wet over there. None of us have been able to ride at all this week.

Anyway, Jim suggested we all go down to the vacant block of land at the end of our street. There's probably a couple of acres there and he walked down this morning to have a look. Luckily for us, it's nowhere near as wet as our paddocks. So we all decided to tack up and go down there for a ride.

I could see that Nikita was really shy because she didn't really know anyone. So I walked along on Sparkle right next to her and Cappy. Mom was chatting with Jo. Then Nikita and I started chatting as well. She goes to a different pony club to me and she was telling me all about it. I told her that my pony club's gymkhana is coming up soon and she said that she'll probably go to that. She said she loves going to gymkhanas.

She said that her pony club is going to have a gymkhana soon as well. She thinks it's maybe a month after mine. Each of the different pony clubs holds their own gymkhana and this means I can go to lots of them this year. This will be so fun. As long as I can get Sparkle on the float!!

Nikita and I had a great time riding around the vacant block together. We just trotted and cantered around and followed each other. Cappy is so little. Everyone loves him. He gets along well with Sparkle too. It's amazing because Nikita told me that he's actually a really good jumper. I'm sure he's really good at sporting because he's so small and quick, but it's hard to imagine such a little pony going over big jumps. I can't wait to see her jump him.

When we got back home and untacked the horses, Nikita

came down to the house with me to look at our baby chickens. She is such an animal lover and I knew that she'd really like to see them. It was so cute, because they'd escaped from the pen Dad made and were down on the grass with Sheba. They've got used to her because she sits by their pen every day. I think she feels like she's their mom. It's really cute!

Nikita is really nice. I think we're going to become good friends!

## Saturday 6 April

Nikita's mom, Jo rang us last Sunday night. She said she's heard about a horse trainer who might be able to come out and help us with loading Sparkle on the float. Apparently he's helped lots of horses with the same problem.

We told Shelley about him as well and her parents were keen to ask him to help Millie too. So Dad called him straight away and arranged for him to come this weekend. We were so glad that he was available. Today, Dad had to go to Tom's to borrow his float so the trainer could use it when he arrived this afternoon.

We couldn't believe how quickly he trained Sparkle! It only took him about 4 goes and she was walking on and off the float without a problem. It was amazing! He got me to practice with her and she was so good. I was able to get her on and off easily!

After he worked with Millie on the float, Shelley asked him to help with getting her across the creek as well. She's too scared to walk over the rocks and always jumps across. But this is so dangerous. Millie is such a scaredy cat and it took him a long time! Eventually, he was able to get her to cross. He said that it doesn't usually take this long when he's working with horses but that every horse is different. Millie is just a big chicken!

The best news is that now, Shelley and I will be able to go to pony club tomorrow because we'll be able to get Sparkle and Millie on the float - easily. The forecast is for fine weather and we can't wait. We're both really excited. It's been a whole month since we last went and we can't wait to go again. Hopefully the rider class instructor will be there. I need to practice for the gymkhana!

## Sunday 7 April

Sparkle walked straight onto the float today – both this morning on the way to pony club and this afternoon when we were leaving. It was easy peasy! I'm so proud of her. Millie still seems a bit scared but when she sees Sparkle go on, then she walks on too.

And it was a really fun day! The rider class instructor was awesome and she was really impressed with my riding. I felt so proud of myself. I also got to go in the same jumping group as Kelly this afternoon. That was really fun because she's a really great girl! Shelley and Kate are usually in different groups to me so I only get to catch up with them during lunch breaks.

The instructor was helping me get Sparkle over the jumps. She's still being a bit stubborn and refuses the jumps sometimes. But I'm improving at being really firm with her and that helps a lot.

At the end of the day, we all hosed our horses down, tied them up and gave them some feed. I gave Sparkle a biscuit of hay as well as some special feed in her bucket. I'm still trying to fatten her up but it's taking a while. Then we got to just hang out in the clubhouse while all the parents sat around and chatted.

I just LOVE pony club. It's the best!

## Monday 6 May

I can't believe a whole month has passed since I've had a chance to write in my diary! I've been so busy working with Sparkle to get her ready for the gymkhana and now it's only 6 days away. Mom has been coming over to the paddock with me every afternoon and timing me on the barrels, bounce pony and bending. Sparkle is getting so much quicker at everything.

I can't wait until next weekend! Shelley and I have decided to spend all day on Saturday getting our horses ready. We're going to bathe them and groom them so their coats are really shiny. Then Shelley's going to show me how to braid Sparkle's mane and tail. Mom's going to buy some maroon and cream ribbon because these are our pony club colors. And I'm going to thread the ribbon through her tail and also her mane. I've got the really pretty maroon and cream brow band that Josh's mom made for me as well. Sparkle is going to look great.

And the great news is, Shelley's parents decided to buy their own float. They ordered it a while ago and it's finally ready for them to pick up. They're going to keep it here at our place and they said that I can use it for Sparkle any time I want. That is nice of them and I'm really lucky!!! Now Dad doesn't have to drive to Tom's house all the time to borrow his. I don't think he was very happy about us using it all the time anyway. So, I'm very lucky that Shelley is getting one of her own. And she's going to keep it here. That will make everything so much easier!

Cammie, Grace and Ali still don't have a float to use – so they can't go anywhere – except walk to the state forest for a trail ride.

I'm lucky - and I can't wait for the weekend!!!!!!

## Saturday 11 May

I loved today. We bathed and groomed the horses and their coats look so shiny now. The braiding took quite a while – Shelley showed Mom and I a special way to braid the mane and it's quite tricky, especially threading the colored ribbon through. I'm glad Mom was helping me. We also painted their hooves with special hoof paint. I used a shiny clear one on Sparkle and her hooves look so much better. Shelley said that some girls even put special make up on their horses. I can't believe that! Make up on a horse!! That's mainly for shows though – when they want to cover up any marks and make their horses look absolutely perfect.

When we finished the grooming – which took us all afternoon - we put their rugs on to keep them nice and clean. This will help to keep the braiding in place as well. And tonight we're keeping them under the house. There's such a big area there that's fenced off, so we can keep them in. I guess it's kind of like a stable and because they're together, they won't get scared. This way, we can keep them from rolling around on the grass or in any mud. So they should still be lovely and clean in the morning.

I need to go and clean all my tack now and get it as shiny as possible.

I can't wait till tomorrow. I'll have to be up really early so that I'm ready in time. I can't wait to wear my special shirt and vest. I'll have to get Dad to do my tie up for me.

## Sunday 12 May

Today was the best day of my life!!! Shelley got here really early this morning and we got all our tack together as well as biscuits of hay and buckets of feed for our babies. Then we loaded Millie and Sparkle onto the float. Thank goodness Sparkle is fine now and goes on and off without any trouble at all. Millie still gets scared but as long as Sparkle goes on first, then she just follows.

When we got to pony club, there were horse trailers everywhere. Luckily no one had taken our special spot, so we were able to park there and tack up next to Kate. I was so excited and we could tell that the horses were getting excited as well. They both looked so beautiful with their manes and tails braided and their shiny coats. I felt so proud in my special competition uniform as well.

First of all we had the march past and all the horses from each club walked around the arena in groups. Our horses looked so smart. The colors of our pony club really stood out and definitely looked the best! Mom said that we deserved to win. It was such a great way to start the day!

Then all the riders had to go into their age groups for the events. Nikita was there competing and so was her mom, Jo. Jo went with the seniors, Nikita went in the Under11's group and I went in the Under 10's group. That's because my birthday is so late in the year and I won't turn 10 until then.

There were 12 riders in my group all from different clubs. I was feeling so nervous and I think Sparkle was nervous too. Mom and Dad were nearby watching and Dad had our video camera. He always has the video camera – he videos everything!

My first event was bending and I was really excited because I know how good Sparkle is at this. When the gun fired, she took off so quickly and we raced around each pole. I knew that I'd gone really fast but we had to wait until everyone had their turn before the winners were announced. They gave out the ribbons straight away…white for 5th place, yellow for 4th, green for 3rd, red for 2nd and blue for 1st. And I was given the green! I was very happy! My very first gymkhana event and I had won a ribbon!!! I felt great!

My next event was bounce pony and Sparkle raced over all the logs without knocking any off. In this event I came 2nd. So I had a green and a red ribbon.

After that it was the keyhole race. I've never done that before, so I waited to go last. This way I could watch the other riders to see how it's done. The first 3 were disqualified because they rode out of the key. I could see that I needed to do sharp turns but Sparkle is really good at those, so I was hoping she'd do well.

When it was finally my turn, we raced down the straight part, around the key hole and then back again. There was so much cheering and I could hear people calling out my name. Ali, Cammie and Grace had turned up to watch and got there just in time to see me go. Nate was there as well as Mom and Dad and they were all cheering me on.

The judge gave me the blue ribbon! I couldn't believe it. Everyone was crowding around me saying congratulations! Another girl even commented to her mom about how lucky I was to have so many people watching me and cheering for me. She told her mum that I had my very own cheer squad. And I guess she was right. I felt really proud!

The next event was jumping. I got really nervous about this one and I guess that Sparkle could sense it. I pushed her on and made sure I looked straight ahead to where I wanted her to go. There were some really good jumpers in my group so it was pretty tough. Sparkle knocked over a jump which made me lose points and she refused a jump as well. I had to turn around and take her towards it again. She went over it the second time, but that slowed me down a fair bit. I didn't get a ribbon for that event, but Dad asked the judge and she said that I had come 6th. Everyone said that this was really impressive for my very first jumping competition. I was so pleased with myself and with Sparkle.

The girl who won the red ribbon for jumping, shocked everyone! When the judge handed it to her, she threw it down on the ground and said - it's not good enough! She then got down off her horse and screamed out – STUPID HORSE! Then she walked off in a big huff. We were all so shocked! We've never seen anything like that before. Her mom had to grab her horse's reins so he didn't run away. I think her mom was really embarrassed. I don't think I'll ever forget that girl. What a way to behave!

There were so many different events and I won ribbons in nearly all of them. Mom was carrying them for me and there were so many. I think my favorite event of the day though was Mystery. A lot of the horses get scared in this because they have to race over all these mysterious surfaces, like plastic tarpaulins and old tyres and also go through steamers and curtains that have been strung up around the trees. But Sparkle is so bomb proof that nothing seems to spook her. I was able to get her through the whole event without any problem. Poor Shelly couldn't even finish it on Millie when her group went through because Millie was so scared. I think she stopped at the plastic tarp and would not go any further. Poor Shelley! Anyway, Sparkle came 2nd so I got another red ribbon. I was really happy!

At the end of the gymkhana was the presentation. This is where they add up all the points that each person gets in their age group. It turned out that I came 4th in my age group overall and I won a trophy!!! I was so excited, I couldn't believe it! My very first gymkhana ever and I won a trophy.

I was happy driving home. We were all talking about it and Mom and Dad were really proud of me. My ribbons and trophies are so pretty – I'm going to put them somewhere special in my room so I can look at them every day. I think I'll take them to school for show and tell tomorrow. I can't wait to show everyone.

I'm proud of my baby! She's the best pony EVER!!!

## Saturday 18 May

Everyone at school loved my ribbons and trophy. Miss Johnson was really interested in the events at the gymkhana and she asked me to explain them all to the class. They thought it was really cool and asked me if I get scared when I jump.

Mom has asked me that as well. I'm not scared but it makes me nervous when Sparkle refuses to go over. I was practicing my jumping today and it wasn't much fun. She kept stopping at the jumps and I had so much trouble trying to get her over any of them. I have to grip so hard because I'm really worried that I'm going to fall off. I've only fallen off her once so far and that's because I was being silly when the girls and I were riding in the paddock one time last year. I was kind of bouncing around in the saddle and laughing and mucking around. And I wasn't holding the reins properly. She kind of made a really quick movement – maybe something spooked her or maybe it was because of me being silly. Anyway, all of a sudden I was on the ground. It really gave me a fright. I didn't hurt myself too much but it was hard not to cry. And I didn't want to get back on.

Ali's mom told me I should though. She said that the best thing is to get straight back up in the saddle. I really didn't want to but all the girls were watching me. I was feeling really embarrassed about it all. They kept asking me if I was alright. But this just made me more embarrassed. In the end, I decided I'd better hop back on – it would be too embarrassing not to!

Mom said that she was really worried when she saw me fall. But at least I wasn't hurt and it certainly taught me a lesson. I'll never be silly on a horse again, that's for sure.

Anyway, it's pony club tomorrow and I'll be able to practice my jumping there. I hope that Sparkle behaves. I'm going to give her some extra special feed tonight to make sure she has plenty of energy.

I can't wait to see everyone.

## Sunday 19 May

I couldn't wait to get there today. Shelley and I were the first to arrive, so we had plenty of time to get the horses tacked up and ready. It was such a beautiful day and I couldn't wait to get started. We've been bringing Sheba to pony club each time we go now. Other people bring their dogs too, but I know that all the girls like Sheba the best! She loves all the attention she gets when she goes there. And the new trick that Dad taught her is so funny. He points his finger as if it's a gun and says – Bang, Bang - then she rolls over onto her back and pretends that she's dead. Everyone loves that trick and they're always trying to get her to do it.

When I hopped on Sparkle, she seemed just as excited as me. I could tell she was looking forward to the day too. We went off into our groups and I did rider class first. I'm working on getting her to use the correct lead when she canters. This is really important and if she's not doing it properly, I'll never do well in that event at gymkhanas. I'm still learning how to get her to do it. And I'm not sure if she is or not, so I have to ask Mom to tell me. The instructor said that when you get really good at it, you can feel the difference when you're riding and you'll know if it's right or not. I'll just have to keep practicing.

We did lots of different training exercises in the different arenas and that was really fun. Then we all stopped for a lunch break. It was such a hot day today, so everyone was glad to have a rest and something to drink and eat. I bet the horses were too.

After lunch, most of the girls chose to do jumping. I was nervous about this because Sparkle's been so naughty at it lately. I managed to get her over the first jump so that made me feel better. It was only a little one though, but it was a good start. They gradually made the jumps higher and Sparkle started off behaving well. I was pushing her on and I could see her ears going forward. I think she was enjoying it too.

Then they raised the jumps some more. But Sparkle was being so good that I felt really confident. I turned her towards the first one and just as we got close she suddenly stopped. I felt myself flying forwards and I had to grip so hard to stop myself from coming off. It was really scary. The instructor told me to try again. I felt really nervous especially with everyone watching. I took her towards the jump and she did exactly the same thing. It was so hard to stay in the saddle and I could feel my thigh muscles aching from gripping so tightly. Then I tried one more time. I think I was expecting it and sure enough, she stopped again. But this time was so sudden, that I could not stay on. I felt myself flying through the air and then I hit the ground. I knocked the jump off with my arm as I fell and came down right on top of it. Everyone came running over to see if I was ok. I felt a bit dazed and my arm really hurt. The worst part though was that it was so embarrassing! I hated everyone staring at me. And it was hard not to cry!

I didn't want to do any more. So I took her out of the ring, untacked her and hosed her down.

She's being naughty and I don't know what to do!

Now I have a really sore arm from where I fell. Dad said that it's a wonder I didn't get seriously injured. He was amazed that I was able to get up and just walk away.

The instructor told him that we should get Sparkle looked at. He said that maybe she has an injury and is in pain or maybe the saddle is hurting her. But it can't be the saddle – it's my new Wintec and I only just got it for my birthday last year!

Someone else said that maybe she's just being naughty and needs a trainer to get her to behave.

Dad said that he's going to call Alice who owns the Andalusian horse property down the end of our street. She's a horse trainer and also a Bowen therapist for horses. Dad said that he'll call to see if she can come and have a look at Sparkle. Apparently Bowen therapy is a special type of massage that even humans can have done when they have sore muscles or problems with their body. Hopefully she'll be able to work out what's wrong.

I wonder if she is sore or if it's the saddle causing all the problems. Or if she's just being naughty!

I hope that Alice can come soon so that Sparkle gets back to normal. I just want her to be the way she used to be!

*This is exactly what happened to me today!!*

## Monday 20 May

This afternoon, I found Sparkle lying down in the paddock. At first I thought she was just resting, but when she saw me she would not get up. And when she sees me with her feed bin, she always comes trotting over. I started to panic. It reminded me of seeing Charlie lying down in his paddock after the snake bite. I thought - Oh no! Not a snake! Not my baby!

I went running over to her, but she wouldn't move. She was breathing. But she just laid there looking at me. My poor Sparkle – I didn't know what to do! I started crying and I could hear myself saying – Sparkle! Sparkle! Please don't die!!!

I didn't want to leave her but there was no one in the paddock to help me. So I had to run down to the house to get Mom and Dad. My heart was thumping so badly, I almost couldn't breathe!

They raced back over to the paddock with me. I couldn't get there quickly enough. As soon as Mom saw Sparkle, she tried calling the vet. But he wasn't available! The other 2 vets we know of were on other calls as well and couldn't come till much later. We couldn't believe it! Mom had to keep trying until she finally found someone else. He told her he would come straight away and that he would be here as quickly as possible. He said we should just stay with Sparkle and keep her calm.

I was in such a panic. I was trying to be strong and not cry. She couldn't die! I wasn't going to let her. I thought if I talk to her it would help. So I ran my fingers through her mane and stroked her neck. I told her how special she is to me and that I can't live without her. I told her that she has to stay strong and get better. I told her that she's the best pony in the world and that I love her.

She just looked at me with her beautiful, big, brown eyes and I knew that she was listening.

Finally the vet came. He said she has an infection because her temperature is really high. But he's not sure what's causing it. He gave her an injection with some really strong antibiotics. He said we should cover her with a rug and just keep her calm. He said that there's nothing else he can do at the moment and that he'll come back in a few hours to check on her again.

I've been sitting with her in the paddock. Mom and Dad kept coming over to check on me - and on Sparkle. Dad finally said I have to come down to the house – he's with her now and he thinks I'm eating dinner.

But I'm not hungry! I don't want dinner – I just want to stay with my baby!

I'm going to go back over now to be with her. The vet should be back soon and I want to be there when he comes.

Sparkle, I love you.

Please get better!!!

## Tuesday 21 May

The nickering I could hear as I tumbled out of bed this morning, had to be Sparkle's. It's amazing how well noise carries across the paddocks and I knew that I would recognize that sound anywhere. She has a different tone to the other horses and I always know when it's her. Mom says it's just like being a parent. They always seem to recognize the sound of their own child's voice above all the others. And it's the same with me and my baby.

The vet finally came back last night after what seemed like hours of waiting. Even though Mom and Dad kept insisting that I go back to the house, there was no way I was going to leave her on her own. The only way they could coax me to get some rest was if Dad promised to stay with her. But I knew I wouldn't get any sleep. How was that going to be possible when my baby was so sick? I didn't even know if she would survive the night!

As I raced over to the paddock this morning, my heart was thumping wildly and the same words kept going around in my head – Please let her be okay! Please let her be okay!

I could not get across the creek and up the hill quickly enough. But when I finally reached the point where I could see her, I just couldn't stop my tears from falling.

I've been having constant visions of Ali's horse Charlie, lying deathly still on the ground after being bitten by a snake earlier this year. He was in such a bad way, that after 3 days of being unable to stand, his muscles completely gave way and he had to be put down. This was my biggest fear with Sparkle when I couldn't get her onto her feet yesterday.

But after a night of rest and several doses of really strong antibiotics, she was actually not only standing but walking towards me! My baby was alive and I knew in my heart that she was going to be ok.

I gently stroked her neck and she nuzzled up to me. I felt so grateful right then. I thought I was the luckiest girl ever! But when the vet came to check on her later this morning, he said that she's been suffering from a serious flu virus. And that she's really lucky to have survived. He said that she's going to need lots of rest and some special attention for a while. I am more than happy to do that for her but I was not prepared for what he told me next.

Her sporting days are over. He said that along with the flu virus, which will take quite a while for her to recover properly from, she's also developed chronic arthritis. And the kindest thing to do would be to retire her in the paddock, with some occasional gentle riding. I couldn't believe what I was hearing! What about pony club? What about competing in gymkhanas? What about improving my jumping? He said all of that will definitely be out of the question for her now. And that she will more than likely refuse if I even try to get her over a jump.

So that explains why she's been so stubborn and naughty lately! It's just been too painful for her to even attempt jumping. I've had no idea! Thank goodness there's some medicine I can give her to help with that now, so that she won't feel so sore. As long as I hardly ride her that is.

I'm so glad she's ok, but what am I going to do? How will I be able to cope without riding? Horses and riding are my entire world now. I have to be able to ride!

After hearing that news, I refused to go to school today! I just wanted to stay with my baby. And I was way too upset to be going anywhere. Mom thought I needed to stay at home and rest, but when I ran into my room, I couldn't stop crying! It's not fair!

## Wednesday 22 May

I hardly slept at all last night and I did not want to go to school again today. But Mom said I had to. When I checked on Sparkle before leaving to catch the bus though, she seemed to be quite content. I wonder if the arthritis medicine is working already. Hopefully it is! The vet said that it's an anti-inflammatory which will help to stop the pain. She was happily grazing when I got home this afternoon as well. It's almost like she was never sick.

When I finished checking her over, I spotted Ali, Cammie and Grace all tacking up to go for a ride. They were planning to practice their jumping but I didn't stay and watch. The thought of it just brought tears to my eyes.

And I know they're planning another trail ride in the state forest on the weekend. But what am I supposed to do? Shelley's keen to go as well, so I guess I'll just be stuck here on my own – unless Nikita comes over to ride Cappy. I hope she does. At least I'll have Sparkle to keep me company. Mom keeps telling me to be grateful that she's still alive. And I am!!! But it's just not the same.

## Thursday 23 May

I can't believe what Mom and Dad are planning! They haven't told me this before, but ever since Sparkle started refusing jumps and being naughty, they've been looking in the paper for another horse that's easier to handle. And now that I really can't ride her much anymore, they said that as soon as her health starts to improve, we need to sell her or give her away. And in the meantime, start looking for another horse.

I can't believe they would even think about doing this! How can I sell my baby? I can't just get rid of her! How can they even think that I would want to do that?

Having 2 horses to look after would cost too much money. That's what Mom and Dad say, anyway. It's not fair! I would love to have a new horse to ride but I have to be able to keep Sparkle!!

What am I going to do?

## Saturday 25 May

The girls all went for a trail ride early this morning. I could hear their voices and laughter when they got back. I'm sure they had the best time. I didn't want to go over there though, it's too upsetting. It's not fair that I can't ride.

I went to check on Sparkle later this morning when no one else was around. She seems to be recovering really well. She was so happy to see me and nuzzled my hands and pockets looking for treats. It's the cutest thing when she does that.

I sat under the big tree and just watched her grazing. Sheba came over to keep me company and laid down in the shade next to me. I'm so lucky to have such a beautiful dog. Everyone adores her! But she sure is getting fat now. It's only a few weeks until her puppies arrive. Mom and Dad suggested a few months ago that we should let her have a litter. And they decided to look for another pure bred golden retriever to breed her with. When we saw how protective of our baby chickens she was, we knew she'd be a great mom. We're sure she thought the chicks were actually her babies. I'm really looking forward to the puppies arriving. A litter of little retriever puppies will be so cute!

I've been thinking a lot today and I've come up with a plan! I'm going to start looking for a new pony. Then I'm going to convince Mom and Dad to let me keep Sparkle as well. I'll do lots of chores so I get more pocket money and I can help pay for her feed. It's the arthritis supplements and special feed for her that cost the most. But I have lots of birthday money saved up, so maybe I can use some of that. And hopefully because Sparkle's getting older, no one will want to take her anyway. I'm sure it'll all work out. Mom always says – you get what you focus on – so that's what I'm going to focus on now…getting a beautiful new pony AND keeping Sparkle.

I think I'll get on the computer right now and check to see what ponies are for sale.

## Sunday 26 May

Last night, I found 3 horses that look like they'll be just perfect. It's really hard because there's so many beautiful ponies for sale but they're either too far away for us to go and look at – some are even in other states – or they're just not the right type of horse for me.

I made a checklist of all the different things I need in a horse.

First of all, I don't want one that's too big or too small. Probably between 14 and 15 hands would be good.

The age is important – somewhere between 8 and 14, I guess. Definitely no older!

I also want a horse that's good at sporting because I LOVE gymkhanas and I really want to go in lots of them this year.

And I want a good jumper, because I'd like to do lots of jumping.

I guess an all-rounder type of horse would be perfect. That way, I'll be able to do lots of different styles of riding. I'd love to try eventing – that would be so cool!

As well as that, I want one that has a nice quiet nature and isn't hard to pull up.

I know that's a lot to ask for, but there are 3 horses on horseyard.com that pretty much fit the description I'm looking for AND they're not too far away. I'm so glad Nikita told me about that site – that's where her mom found her latest horse and she's so happy with him.

Sparkle has become hard work lately and even though I haven't wanted to admit this before, it hasn't been a lot of fun riding her. Cammie and Grace's dad, Jim says I should get a gelding. He says that they are definitely much calmer to work with and have less attitude than mares.

Anyway, the 3 horses that I've picked out actually are geldings and they look so pretty as well. Mom said that she'll call the owners tonight and have a chat with them. Hopefully, we'll be able to go and have a look on the weekend.

This is really exciting! I can't wait!!

## Wednesday 29 May

Mom's managed to speak to the owners of all 3 horses that I picked out. One of the ponies sold on the weekend, which is a shame because he sounded really nice. But we're going to look at the other 2 on Saturday.

I really hope that one of them is the horse for me. Pony club is on Sunday but I can't go because I don't have a horse to ride. So the sooner I find one, the better!

**Saturday 1 June**

I was so excited for today, but then in the car, I started getting really nervous. It's kind of scary hopping on horses that you don't know and then having people stand around watching you ride. It's really nerve-wracking! You kind of feel like they're judging your riding while they're watching you.

Anyway, maybe Beau picked up on the way I was feeling. That's the first horse I tried. The owners told us that he's like a big teddy bear, but he certainly wasn't like that for me, that's for sure. He started pig rooting and being really naughty. I got scared and had to hop off. Mom and Dad told the owner, that he's probably not right for me. I wouldn't want him anyway! It's amazing what people say when they're trying to sell their horses. Beau was definitely no teddy bear! He was even naughty for the owner when she hopped on him. And then she tried to make excuses for why he was behaving like that.

We've heard horror stories about what some owners do. Sometimes they even drug their horses so they're well-behaved when people try them out. But then when they get them home, they go psycho!! It's pretty scary when you think about it. You have to be so careful when you're buying a horse.

The next horse was named Duke. And that name suited him so much. Mom said that he was kind of regal looking and knew that he was beautiful. The girl who owns Duke used to show him and did quite well but now she has a new horse that's a really good jumper. That's what she wants to get into.

Duke was lovely to ride and seemed like he had a really nice nature. And he was gorgeous looking as well. But he's not a sporting pony – he's definitely meant for the show ring. Mom and Dad were annoyed because we drove so far and wasted a whole day looking at horses that were nothing like what I wanted. It's such a shame that the other one sold. I bet he would have been perfect.

Now I have to keep looking for something else. I hope I can find a pony soon. I'll have to try some other websites and Dad said that he'll check the paper.

Fingers crossed – we'll find the perfect pony this week. I hope so anyway!

## Wednesday 5 June

The most amazing thing happened tonight! Dad opened the local paper and found a 14.2 hand, 11 year old, chestnut all-rounder advertised for sale. He said he wasn't actually planning to look for horses, but for some reason, the ad just seemed to jump out at him.

Anyway, when he rang the owner, he could not believe who he was speaking to! It turned out to be Josh's mom, Tracey. They're the people who we bought Sparkle off! What a coincidence!! Mom said that it's just meant to be! Tracey is the nicest lady ever and she was really helpful when we were buying Sparkle. She said that she's really sad to be selling Tara – that's the horse's name - but Josh just doesn't ride anymore. She said that Tara's going to waste in their paddock and that she's way too good a horse for that.

And the best part is, she sounds PERFECT!!!!

I know she's a mare, but Tracey says that she's absolutely beautiful and has the nicest nature ever.

We're going to look at her tomorrow afternoon.

I'm SO excited!!

TARA! TARA! TARA! TARA! TARA! TARA! TARA! TARA!

What a lovely name!

She's going to be the one!

I JUST KNOW IT!!!

## Thursday 6 June

Tara is the loveliest horse! As soon as I hopped on her, I knew straight away that she was going to be perfect. She's really calm, has a lovely soft mouth and is really easy to pull up. I tried her over some jumps and she didn't even hesitate. I think she's going to be a perfect all-rounder. And Tracey says that she's totally suitable for beginners right through to advanced riders. She's an ideal size for me as well and even as I get taller, she won't be too small. I love her gentle nature - I can see why Tracey is sad to be selling her.

And she's really good at sporting. Tracey showed us the trophies and ribbons that Josh and Tara have won in gymkhanas. There's heaps of them!! That is so cool!

As well as all of that, Tracey said that Tara is a very good doer! She's really rounded and easily keeps weight on just by grazing in the paddock. They hardly have to give her any extra feed at all. This is great! Especially with all the money it costs us to feed Sparkle.

After Mom and Dad chatted with Tracey for a while, they suddenly decided to pay a holding deposit. It all happened so quickly. Mom was reluctant to decide straight away, but they could see how much I love her and how perfect she is. And they were also worried she might sell. There's a lady wanting to look at her on the weekend - it would be terrible if she was sold to someone else. Anyway, we're going back tomorrow for another look, just to be sure.

Tracey said that she would love to have had a daughter who is horse mad like me. Josh is a good rider but she said he always preferred motorbikes.

Tara is SO pretty! I really don't know how he can sell her, but I'm glad he is. Tracey said that the money will go straight into his bank account. I wonder if he'll spend it on a new bike?

Oh my gosh! I know this is going to work out perfectly. I'm getting a beautiful new pony called Tara. This is a dream come true.

I'm going to call the girls right now and tell them all. I can't wait for them to see her! Tracey said that she can bring her to our house on Saturday.

I CAN'T WAIT!!!!!

## Saturday 8 June

I can't believe that I actually have a new pony!

I was really excited when Tracey unloaded her this afternoon. She is just beautiful! And she goes on and off the float easily. She crossed the creek without any trouble as well. I put her in the small paddock next to Sparkle and Millie, just so they can adjust to each other over the fence. They were so cute – they walked over to say hello to her straight away – I'm sure they'll all get along really well.

I think Tracey was really sad to say goodbye. Mom said that she thought Tracey was going to cry. She's keen to watch us compete in some gymkhanas, so at least she'll still get to see Tara. And she's going to make me some more brow bands as well. That's so nice of her! She's such a nice lady! I told her that I'll call and let her know how Tara is going. She's really glad that we've bought her – she said she knows that Tara will be in good hands.

I spent the rest of the afternoon in the paddock, just watching her graze. I'm going to have to be careful not to neglect Sparkle now – or she might get jealous. Ali, Cammie and Grace all came over to see my new pony and they think she's beautiful as well. I can't wait to show Shelley and Nikita. And I can't wait to go riding on her! I thought I should just let her settle in today and give her time to get used to her new home.

I still adore Sparkle and she'll always be my baby, but she has such a quick little trot and is quite hard to pull up. Tara seems a lot easier to ride.

I'm the luckiest girl ever!!

## Sunday 9 June

I had so much fun today. Tara is absolutely awesome!!! I just love her!

She's so easy to pull up and really willing to do whatever I ask her. I tried her with bending and bounce pony and she's really good at both of them. And it was lovely to jump her as well. She didn't shy away from the jumps even once. Her ears go straight forward and I'm sure she loves jumping as much as me.

Her trot is perfect too and really easy to rise to. I just love riding her.

Nikita came over today with her mom Jo and they were very impressed. Jo asked me all about her and wanted to know where I'd found her – as soon as she saw her, she commented on how lovely she is.

I felt so proud.

She really is a dream pony.

I can't wait to take her to pony club next weekend. They're all going to love her too, I know it!!

## Monday 10 June

Shelley came over this afternoon and we rode in the big paddock together. Tara was really well-behaved and Shelley's very impressed with her. I knew she would be.

After my ride, I put Tara and Sparkle in the paddock together and they just couldn't wait to be near each other. They seem to get on really well. I think they've already become attached. It's crazy though – Tara's much bigger and rounder than Sparkle but I hardly have to feed her at all. Tracey told me how much to give her and I couldn't believe it! Sparkle has to have nearly a full bucket of feed every night plus a biscuit of hay twice a day as well. But Tara only needs a small amount each night, or she might get too fat. The complete opposite of Sparkle! I'm giving Tara hay as well though! I can't give some to Sparkle and not Tara – that wouldn't be fair.

I'll always love Sparkle – she's my first pony and she's very special. But Tara is definitely my dream pony. And I know I'll get to keep them both!

I'm so happy!!!!

## Wednesday 12 June

The most incredible thing happened yesterday afternoon. Mom got home from work and went looking for Sheba. We've been keeping a close check on her lately because we knew the puppies would be due soon - Mom actually thought that there was one more week to go. Anyway, she finally found Sheba in her kennel and when she called her, she wouldn't come out. So Mom said that she bent down to look inside and make sure she was okay. And when she did, she got the surprise of her life. Sheba was having her puppies!! Right then, right while Mom was watching. How incredible is that! I wish we were at home then, but we hadn't got home from school yet. I'm glad in a way that we were late though, because one of them died. Mom said that it was stillborn. That is so sad. That poor little puppy. When Dad came home, she got him to take it away before we saw it.

But the good news is, Sheba has 9 of the cutest little puppies you've ever seen in your entire life!!!! I don't think there could be anything cuter than golden retriever puppies. And 9 of them! Oh my gosh, Sheba is going to be really busy and so are we! We had to move them into a special enclosure that Dad had ready. That was where they were supposed to be born, but I guess Sheba felt more comfortable having them in her kennel.

One of them is sick though. Dad said that there's often a runt in every litter. But we're going to try to save him. He's so little and sweet and we have to make sure that he gets his turn at feeding. All the other pups just barge their way in so they don't miss out. But he's too weak to look after himself. I hope that we can save him and I'm really glad that Mom and Dad want to try. They're even setting the alarm tonight, so they can get up and make sure he gets fed.

Luckily we've been collecting newspapers for a while because we're sure going to need a lot. 9 puppies make a lot of mess! I've had to change the newspaper 4 times already today and I'll have to do it again before I go to bed. At least I was allowed to have the day off school. Mom and Dad said because this is such a special occasion, we should all have the day off.

This is so cool and I can't wait to show the girls. Nikita is especially going to love them. I think she's the biggest animal lover of all of us – except for maybe Shelley. She absolutely adores our pets – she's not allowed to have a cat or a dog because her dad's allergic to their hair. So she loves coming to our place to play with Sheba and Soxy. Wait till she sees the puppies!

I'd better go and check on them.

I hope we don't run out of newspaper!

## Thursday 13 June

I did not want to go to school today! I just wanted to stay with Sheba and her pups. They are really, really cute. I can't believe how cute they are! And Sheba is such a protective mom. She watches every move we make. So we can't take them too far away from her just yet. They still have their eyes closed and they're just adorable. It's keeping me really busy though, because each pup has to be weighed every day. This is to make sure they're putting on weight and getting enough milk. It's impossible to tell them apart though, so we've had to put different colored wool around their necks. I made up a chart today to keep a record of who is gaining weight and how much they've grown. The hardest part was thinking of names for them all! It was very hard to come up with 9 different names.

Tina is what we've called the little one and she's hardly growing at all. Whereas all the others have grown heaps already. I hope that she survives – it would be really sad if she doesn't.

The girls came over to have a look and they think that they're just gorgeous. Nikita stayed all afternoon after her ride. We're becoming such good friends and tomorrow we're going to have a ride together. I'm really looking forward to that!

## Friday 14 June

Nikita and I rode together in the big paddock this afternoon and practiced our jumping. Cappy's so little and cute. It's incredible that he can jump the height that he does! I think Nikita cleared almost 36 inches on him today.

I can't wait to take Tara to pony club on Sunday. I wish Nikita and I went to the same one. That would be awesome if we did.

I got some bad news tonight though! Well, it's terrible for me! When Jo came to pick Nikita up, she told us they're moving their horses on the weekend. I couldn't believe it when I heard! There's not enough grass in our front paddock so Jo has found somewhere else to keep them. Just when Nikita and I have started becoming close and having heaps of fun together. And Cappy is the cutest little pony – I don't want him to go either!

I'm really sad about this. I was hoping that we could go riding together all the time. Nikita is my age and we get on really well. It'd be okay if we went to the same pony club, but we don't.

Dad told Jo that us girls will have to get together sometime and Jo agreed. Hopefully we'll be able to ride again soon. I'm really going to miss Nikita and Cappy! We'll all miss Cappy. I don't think I've ever seen a pony as cute as him!

## Saturday 15 June

It was the funniest thing ever today! Mom, Dad and I all told Nate that he should have a ride on Tara. He wasn't that keen because he's tried riding Sparkle – he even had a couple of lessons – but he didn't really enjoy it very much. I think it's because she's so forward moving and hard to pull up at times, so he was probably a bit scared. But Tara is very different. As Tracey said, she's perfect for any level of rider, including beginners. So after a bit of coaxing, he finally agreed.

The problem is that we don't have a riding helmet to fit him. He has such a big head and there's no way he can get my helmet on. When he rode Sparkle, he borrowed one off the instructor. After that, Mom said there's no point buying one for him if he's not going to ride. So anyway, because he didn't have one to wear today, he wore his motor bike helmet. And it looked so funny!!! We were all cracking up laughing. But Nate didn't care – he was actually having the time of his life. He got so confident, that he tried to get her to canter. That didn't last long though. I don't think he was too sure of that. And it was really funny watching him trying to do a rising trot.

After a while, he decided to even try some small jumps. Tara was just brilliant. She is so willing to do whatever her rider asks of her, that this wasn't a problem at all. And because Nate is such a dare devil and used to going over massive jumps on his motor bike, he thought jumping a horse was great fun!

But I know it's because he was riding my dream pony. I'm becoming so attached to her. She's not only beautiful on the outside, but she's so gorgeous on the inside as well. No wonder Tracey didn't want to sell her!

I think I should call Tracey tonight and let her know how well it's all going. She'll be pleased to hear how happy Tara is, I'm sure.

I also need to get my tack cleaned ready for pony club tomorrow. I definitely want Tara to look her best when we walk into the arena.

I can't wait to get there!!!

*She's so beautiful!!!*

## Sunday 16 June

Today was absolutely awesome! As soon as I arrived, Kate's dad, Tom came straight over to look at Tara. And he was SO impressed. He told me I have a really good horse now and that she would be an excellent endurance pony. That's what he loves doing and said that he'd love to take her on an endurance ride himself. I didn't know much about this before, but apparently they go on rides for miles and miles and ride all day long – with a few rests along the way of course. Sometimes they even camp overnight with the horses and then continue riding for the whole next day. He said that Tara would be a great endurance horse.

So I guess this means that she won't find pony club tiring and I'll be able to do lots of riding on her without wearing her out. This is another great thing about her!

I felt very proud when I walked her into the arena. Her coat looked really glossy and shiny in the sun and my tack was perfectly clean. The instructors always check to make sure we've tacked up properly and I got a perfect score for my tack today. These marks go towards presentation night at the end of the year. I hope I win something!

My first class today was rider class. This is something I've been working on for a while with Sparkle. It's amazing how much easier it is to get it right on Tara though. The instructor kept commenting on how good I looked and how much I've improved. But I still have to work on my canter leads. Sometimes I'm on the right lead and sometimes not. We'll have to keep practicing those.

All through the morning, everyone was commenting on my new pony and saying how nice she is. The instructors were really happy to see me on such a good horse. I was having the best time!

When we did some sporting events in the afternoon, Tara was really quick and even managed to win the bounce pony. That was really cool! And when we did jumping, I wasn't nervous or worried at all. I'm not doing big jumps yet, but she is very willing and I already feel much more confident than I used to.

And to top it all off – Tara walked straight onto the float in the afternoon. Shelley's horse Millie still gets scared, but seeing Tara go straight on, made her feel safe I guess, then she walked on easily as well.

But poor Sparkle was left at home on her own in the paddock today. And she certainly didn't like it when Shelley and I took Tara and Millie out this morning. She wanted to come too and I was a bit worried about leaving her. Luckily though, the other girls' horses are in Ali's paddock, so she could still see them over the fence.

I think she would freak out if we left her completely by herself. It's amazing how quickly the horses have become so attached to each other. It's really beautiful to see.

I love my babies!

And I had the best day ever!!

*Kate's friend…her first time on a horse!*

## Wednesday 19 June

I've been so busy! Having a new horse to ride and 9 puppies to help look after is really hectic. I also have a gymkhana coming up in a couple of weeks so I've been trying to ride Tara as much as possible to get ready for it. I'm sure we'll do well in the sporting but I'd love to win rider class – that would be really cool!

I'm glad that I have another day of pony club before the gymkhana so I can practice with the instructor some more. She is so helpful and she's taught me heaps! I've been working on Tara's canter leads and Mom seems to think that I'm usually on the right one now. A bit more practice and I think we'll be ready.

We were late getting home this afternoon though, because we had to stop in at the local newspaper office to get more newspaper for Sheba and her pups. Luckily they had stacks that they could give us – we're definitely going to need it!

The puppies are getting bigger and fatter and even cuter than ever. I didn't think they could get any more adorable but they actually are! But poor little Tina – she hasn't grown and we're really worried that she may not live. She still drags herself along and tries to get her share of milk. And we still have to make a space for her at feed times, or she'd never get fed. And we got some bad news today, the vet said that she'll probably have to be put down.

That is so sad! How can we have her put down? Poor Sheba! Imagine losing another one of her babies!

## Friday 21 June

Tina died last night. It was so sad when we woke up and found her this morning especially when we saw Sheba licking her and gently prodding her with her paw. I started crying and Nate did too. We went out and buried her in the paddock. We found a special place under a tree and Nate made a little cross for her grave this afternoon after school.

Mom said that it was good we had to go to school because it would take our minds off it. I thought about it all day long though. I didn't want to concentrate on school and I felt really sad – I still do.

Thank goodness the other 8 puppies are so healthy and strong. We just have to really look after Sheba now. Feeding all those pups is really hard on her and she's started losing weight and looking exhausted. It's such a big job! Dad stocked up on extra special feed for her today to give her energy and put some weight back on. We'll have to feed her lots more than usual. I'm sure she'll enjoy that. She loves her food that's for sure.

At one of my parties a couple of years ago, we had a sausage sizzle and Dad left a huge plate of leftover sausages on the brick wall by the pool. Not many had been eaten because everyone was having too much fun in the pool. The mistake he made was that he hadn't thought about Sheba! She got to that plate and ate every single one of those sausages. There must have been 20-30 of them and she ate them ALL. She could barely walk afterwards and her stomach was HUGE!! We had to put her on a diet after that!

## Sunday 23 June

I've spent this weekend, riding Tara around the big paddock – getting her fit and muscly and training her for the gymkhana as well. There's been no one around to ride with though. I don't know what all the other girls have been up to, but I've been on my own in the paddock – with my babies of course. But it's not the same as having a friend to ride with! I wish Nikita and Cappy were still agisting here.

I'm glad I've got the gymkhana to focus on and the puppies of course. They're sure keeping me busy! It's going to be so hard to sell them when they're old enough. Mom and Dad are thinking about keeping one. That would be really special if we could. Imagine that – having Sheba and one of her puppies to play with. That would be great for Sheba when we're all out at school and work each day. She does have our cat, Soxy at home with her but he just tends to sleep the whole time. Once we came home and found the 2 of them asleep together. Soxy was curled up on Sheba's bed right next to her. He couldn't have got closer if he'd tried. But the funny part was, that he was right in the middle of her comfy bed and there was no room for Sheba, so she was sleeping mainly on the floor. Soxy thinks he's the boss, I'm sure of it!

## Saturday 6 July

I could not believe what happened today! The top part of my leg is now pure purple!!! I've never seen such a massive bruise before!

When I went into the paddock this afternoon to get Tara and tack her up, Millie came over and suddenly kicked out towards us. Something must have scared her or she didn't want me near Tara, because she just came over and kicked. I happened to be right in the line of fire and her hoof lashed into my thigh.

I could hear myself scream. It was really weird because it was like I was watching the whole thing happen. But it was actually really happening to me. And all I know is that I've never felt anything so painful before! I collapsed on the ground and couldn't stand up, the pain was that bad. I just had to lie down holding onto my thigh.

Mom came running over calling– Are you alright? Are you alright? She sounded really scared. This has happened to her once before as well, so she knows exactly what it's like.

Ali's horse, Charlie was grazing in our big paddock one time last year and Mom went to catch Sparkle for me. Then all of a sudden, Charlie kicked out at her and managed to get her right in the shin. I remember being so worried about Mom when that happened, because she screamed but then she couldn't talk. She just kind of keeled over, holding her leg.

And the worst part was that because it broke the skin and caused a cut, she ended up with blood poisoning. This is because there's so many germs in a horse paddock and the germs from Charlie's hoof got into Mom's bloodstream. She had to have about a week off work and almost had to go to hospital. Her foot swelled up so much, it looked like a football and she had to stay in bed with it elevated. Any time she wanted to stand and lower her leg, the pain was so incredible, she said it almost made her feel like passing out! It took a whole week before she could walk again and the doctor said that she was very lucky as it could've been extremely serious.

So when Mom saw me lying on the ground after being kicked by Millie, she started to panic. A kick from a horse can cause terrible injuries and we've heard of one girl who was kicked in the back and ended up in a wheelchair!

At first I couldn't talk. It reminded me of seeing Mom doing exactly the same thing when she was kicked. Then all I could think of was the gymkhana tomorrow! How am I going to be able to ride properly after this? I have to go to the gymkhana – it's my first one on Tara and I've been really, really looking forward to it!!!

Mom raced back to the house to get some ice and that helped a lot. After about 20 minutes with the ice on my leg, I told her that I was ready to ride. I had to train for the gymkhana tomorrow and there was no way I was going to let a horse kick stop me - even with a massive bruise on my thigh, the perfect shape of a horse shoe. I'm very lucky though that it's more to the side of my thigh because when I hopped in the saddle, I found that I don't actually put pressure on it when I sit. Otherwise I really don't think I'd be able to compete tomorrow. Shelley will be so upset when she hears. That Millie! She can be such a problem sometimes!! Mom's just relieved that all I've ended up with is a bruise and not a broken leg or much worse than that!

Then after my training session, I had to bathe Tara as well. It's been a full on afternoon, but I have to make sure she's looking shiny and clean. She's such a pretty pony, I'm sure I'll get a ribbon in best presented, especially if I also clean my tack really well tonight. And I'll get up early in the morning so I can braid her mane and tail. I'm getting much better at it now and it doesn't take me very long anymore. It'd be good if Mom could help, but she's hopeless at braiding. She even has trouble doing my plaits for school each day.

Anyway, I'm glad it was Nate's turn to clean up after the puppies tonight. I've got too many other things to do. But I had to write about what happened today while it's still fresh in my mind. I think the photo Mom took says it all though! I never want that to happen to me again, that's for sure!

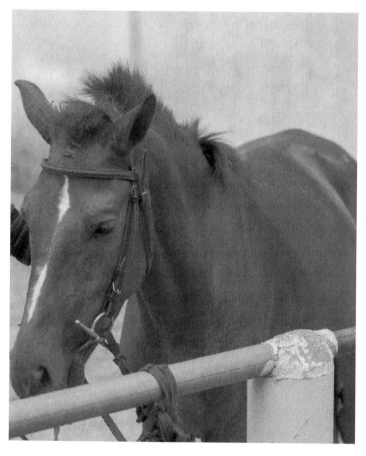

*I still can't believe that Millie kicked me!*

## Sunday 7 July

I was really excited this morning! It was tricky getting to sleep last night though because every time I rolled onto my right side where the bruise is, it woke me up. It does feel very, very sore if I bump it or even try to run around. But thank goodness, it's fine when I'm sitting still. Because I had an incredible day today – bruise and all!

We arrived at the gymkhana nice and early so I would have time to groom Tara, paint her hooves with hoof oil and braid her tail. I'm so glad I have Mom and Dad to help me!! I decided not to worry about her mane. I just did a small braid in her forelock and threaded some maroon and cream ribbon through it. Then when Mom went to fill Tara's water bucket, she bumped into Robin, who is one of the moms from pony club. Robin happened to be braiding the tail of her daughter's horse and when mom commented on what a beautiful job she was doing, she offered to braid Tara's tail as well. I couldn't believe my luck, because she's an expert at braiding and Tara's tail ended up looking so professional! It was much better than what I could have done, that's for sure! I then decided to do a checker pattern on her rump using a nit comb. I've seen other girls doing this and it looks really cool. Tara looked so beautiful when she was finally tacked up and ready. And I felt really proud!!

We went in the march past and our club came second overall – we're very lucky to have such nice uniforms that really stand out. Plus we all had such beautifully groomed horses as well! Then everyone went off into their separate age groups. First of all was best presented and I was thrilled because Tara got the blue ribbon. It was such a great start to the day! She really did look gorgeous though. And the extra time I spent cleaning my tack and boots last night obviously paid off.

It was perfect timing as well because Josh's mom, Tracey arrived just in time to see me win first place. She had told me she was going to try and come, so it was awesome to see that she could make it. I was using the brow band she made me as well. The pony club colors looked gorgeous across Tara's forehead and I know Tracey was pleased to see me using it. I told her that helped us to win – I think she liked that! But I know she was definitely happy to see that Tara is being well looked after.

The first event was bounce pony and Tracey said that Josh always did very well on her in this. I started to feel a bit nervous though because Tracey was watching. I tried to push her on and get her speed up, but she seemed a bit sluggish and I ended up coming 5th. It was great to get another ribbon, but I would have like to have done better – especially with Tracey there.

The next event was barrels and before I had my turn, Tracey gave me some tips that Josh always used when he was competing. She said that this really helped to get Tara going. Before my turn, I had to canter her around in a nearby space a few times to get her psyched up and ready to race. Then as I took off for my turn in the event, I had to give her a good tap with my crop and say – YAH!! YAH!! YAH!! And this worked brilliantly, because I WON!!

I was almost jumping for joy in the saddle! We'd won ribbons in every event so far and I already had 2 blues!

The next event for my age group was rider class. And I really started to get nervous as soon as I realised that! I've been working very hard for this event and I desperately wanted to do well. There were 14 girls in my age group and some really good riders – I remembered them from the last gymkhana. But then I saw who the judge was! It was Keith Lunn. He came as a special guest instructor to our pony club once and everyone was raving about how good he is. Just the sight of him made me even more nervous!

Anyway, because there were so many of us, we all had to do a few laps around the arena, following Keith's instructions while he watched us. Then he asked some people to leave. I was relieved when I realized that I was being asked to stay and continue. At that stage, there were 8 of us left, but obviously only 5 ribbons to be given out. First of all, we had to trot and then go into a canter. I knew that Tara had been on the right lead earlier, which was why we were given another turn. And I was concentrating really hard on making sure that she did that again. I was fairly confident that she was doing it right. At least, I really hoped so, anyway! Then, when he told us all to stop, we had to wait while he decided who should be given ribbons. He gave the white to a girl on a pretty grey mare and then handed the yellow to the girl beside her. After that he headed back up the line towards me and I was sure he was going to hand me the green but he walked straight past. I started to feel sick then, because there were only 2nd and 1st place ribbons to go. All I could think was – is it possible that I could've come 2nd? But then he walked back past me and handed it to a girl on a beautiful chestnut gelding that looked like he belonged in the show ring. My heart sank! It was all I'd been looking forward to and the one ribbon I really wanted to take home – even a white or yellow one for this event would have made me happy!

But then all of a sudden, he was handing the blue to me! I just couldn't believe it was happening! Mom said later that the smile on my face was priceless. She said that she'd been feeling sick with nerves just watching me – and she wasn't even the one riding. But I guess she knew how much it meant and how hard I've been working! Bruise and all – I managed to actually win rider class. I was over the moon!

The mother of the girl who came 5th even congratulated me which was really nice and commented on how lovely my new pony is. She said that she remembered me from the last gymkhana when I was riding Sparkle. The girl who came 3rd congratulated me as well. She was in my group last time and we've kind of become friends. Mom, Dad and Tracey were all raving on about it. I felt so proud!! I don't think I'll ever forget that moment!!!

I then took Tara over to the trailer for a well-deserved lunch break. Just as I started to untack her, we heard on the loud speakers that the Champion Rider event was being held and that all rider class winners had to go to the show ring. This was such a shock because I certainly hadn't been expecting to have to do this. So then I had to quickly get my saddle and bridle back on Tara and race back over to the show ring.

Oh my gosh! I thought I was nervous for rider class but this sure did beat that a hundred times over. I had so many butterflies going around in my stomach that I could hardly ride properly! The ring was full of huge horses and because I'm in one of the younger age groups, there were heaps of older riders and even some ladies in the ring with me as well. And their horses looked spectacular! It was so scary! Even Mom said afterwards that it looked really intimidating.

Just as we all transitioned to a canter, the judge asked us to hand gallop and I had no idea what she was talking about! So all I could do was try to copy the others.

Thank goodness Tracey had left by then because I was really glad she wasn't watching – that would've been even more embarrassing! I'm going to have to ask about the hand gallop when I go to pony club next week – just in case I'm ever asked to do it again. Anyway, I certainly wasn't expecting a ribbon in that event and I was kind of relieved to be asked to leave the ring. It was good to get out of there!

But then just as we managed to sit down and have a rest and some lunch, we heard the call that the afternoon program was beginning. So I had to quickly finish eating, get Tara tacked up again and race over to the jumping ring.

When I got there though, the girls had just finished walking the course with the judge, so I missed out on that. I simply had to line up with the other riders and wait for my turn. When I was called in to start, I headed straight for the first jump and cleared it. That really helped me to feel confident about the rest of them. I then managed to get around the course and only knocked one jump off. Dad said that Tara just clipped it with her hoof, which was a shame as she had pretty much cleared it easily. I really enjoyed that event and felt I'd done very well, but just as I was heading out of the ring, the judge called me over to tell me I was disqualified. I couldn't believe what I was hearing! How could I be disqualified? She told me that I hadn't gone through the start gate and that caused instant disqualification. I felt like crying! It wasn't fair! I told her that I hadn't been able to walk the course and wasn't told about it. But she said there was nothing she could do and I had to leave the ring.

So I just had to stand and watch the rest of the riders compete and then be given their ribbons at the end. I was so upset! I couldn't believe that had happened to me. And I still feel really upset thinking about it even now! Mom said, that at least I've learnt what to do and that I'll never make that mistake again. That doesn't help much though. It was really disappointing!!!!

After that it was time for the mystery event which Tara did not like at all! Sparkle was one of the few horses that would easily walk through all the scary bits and pieces, but I couldn't even get Tara over the plastic that was laid on the ground at the start. Let alone the streamers they had hanging down. There was no way she was going to go through those! Dad suggested that we put some up in the paddock to get her used to them, so she's not so frightened. We might try and do that this week then I can start practicing on her. I should probably put plastic down for her to walk over as well. It's amazing what horses are scared of. They're such big animals but they really are huge scaredy cats. Most of them, anyway!

But regardless of the jumping and mystery events, I still came home with 5 ribbons overall which is such a great result and I even got a pink one. I'd had my eye on those all day but only some judges were giving them out, kind of like an encouragement award. And I ended up getting a pink for flags which is an event I've never done before. So that was really cool.

Then I got the surprise of my life, because at the presentation at the very end of the day, I was given a trophy for coming 4th in my age group overall. I couldn't believe it when my name was announced. That really made up for being disqualified for jumping. I was so happy – it was such a fantastic end to the day!!

What a wonderful dream pony I have. She is just awesome to ride and to compete on. She didn't do anything naughty at all – oh, except refuse to go in the Mystery event. But that's okay – we'll just work on that one.

I gave her some extra feed tonight when we got home. She certainly deserved it! And she didn't even seem tired – I really think she could have kept on going.

I know that I'll sleep well tonight though. I'm exhausted!

## Monday 8 July

This morning at school, Miss Johnson took us down to the oval for our morning run. She's a fitness freak and wants us all to get really fit, like her. She says it also helps us to learn better when we go back to class and is a really great way to start the day. I don't usually mind too much, because I want to get fit. But I just knew that it would hurt because of my bruise!

So when I told her that I couldn't run today because I have a bruise, she just laughed at me and told me to get going. When I told my best friend Tina, she said – You have to show her! She doesn't understand! – Tina was in shock when I showed her earlier this morning. Of course she was tempted to poke at it and that really did hurt. Anyway, the thought of having to run around the oval 3 times was just too much, so I decided to pull up the leg of my shorts so Miss Johnson could see what I was talking about.

It was actually really funny to watch her jaw drop! She said – OH MY GOSH!!!! You really DO have a bruise!!!!! How on earth did you do that?

When I explained what had happened, she quickly told me I'd better go and sit down. So at least it got me out of running, I guess!

Anyway, I've been thinking about Tara and the mystery event and Dad said that he has some old black plastic that I can use. So we're going to cut it up and hang it off one of the branches of the big tree in the paddock. I'm looking forward to seeing what she thinks of that!

Now I need to go and put some fresh newspaper down for the pups. They're definitely getting bigger and noisier. I can even hear them from my room. At least we all get to cuddle them on our laps now while we're watching TV at night. And they are so cuddly!!

*Aren't they beautiful!!*

## Thursday 11 July

Well, we're going to need lots of practice walking Tara through the streamers. She's not keen on them at all and insisted on just going around when we tried her this afternoon. We're just going to leave them attached to the tree for now and hopefully she'll get used to them eventually.

She wasn't too bad with the plastic on the ground though. It took a bit of patience, but in the end, I got her to walk over it.

I just love her!!!

## Sunday 21 July

I don't think anything can compare to doing what we did today!!!

Jo and Nikita invited me to go with them to the lake that's not too far from our house. They go riding there all the time and Nikita's told me how much fun it is to ride horses in water. She said the horses love it too. It was so nice that Nikita asked me to come along. I haven't seen her since they moved their horses out of our front paddock and I've really been missing her.

So we got up early and met them down at the lake. Mom and Dad helped me unload Tara and tack her up then they arranged to meet us back at the same spot later in the morning. I had my favorite pink horsey T shirt on and I was so excited!

We had to go along a trail first which led to the lake. And, oh my goodness. Words can't describe how beautiful it looked at 6:30 this morning!!! The sun was rising over the crystal, clear water which was just like a sheet of glass! It was the most perfect day and one of the most beautiful views I've ever seen!

The water was only about a foot deep along the edge and the horses were able to splash around in it. Because it was quite shallow, it wasn't a struggle for them to move through it. This must have felt really good because they absolutely loved it! Then we started cantering, their hooves splashing up water all around me. It was definitely the best feeling in the whole world! It felt like I was flying!

But then I happened to look down in the water and screamed. Tara had almost stepped on a sting ray that was swimming past us. That was freaky!

After a while, we went back through the bush and onto a jumping track where some of the trails had little logs that we could jump over. So we cantered through and it was SO much fun. At the end of the track, we had to keep them moving so the lactic acid didn't build up in their joints after all the cantering and jumping.

Then we slowed down to a walk and passed a paddock where a donkey was grazing. It was quite funny, because Tara became startled when she saw it. It was like she was saying – What's that scary thing?? It really made me laugh. She's such a cutie!

When we headed back through the water, I ended up being in the lead alongside Jo. I asked if we could canter and then the horses started racing each other. I called out to Jo - Can we gallop? And it was the most magical feeling in the entire world. The water was so clean and clear, we could even see the sand at the bottom.

I don't think I've ever experienced the feeling I had today. Galloping through that lake is the highlight of my life so far! It was AMAZING!!!

I want to go again tomorrow!!!!

## Sunday 28 July

It was pouring with rain again this morning so pony club was cancelled. There's been rain on and off all week but I was hoping that it would stop for today. I was really looking forward to going. At least the rain stopped this afternoon though, so I got to have a ride in the small paddock at least – it tends to stay drier than our big paddock, which is lucky.

Tara didn't seem to be herself today. Maybe the bad weather is making her cranky. The paddock was pretty wet anyway, so I only had a short ride.

I hope that it's fine next Sunday because Pony Club has been rescheduled for then.

I'll have to pray for good weather!

## Friday 1 August

Finally the sun came out today! I was so glad because today is Tara and Sparkle's birthday. Well, I don't actually know which day they were born exactly, but every horse has their birthday on 1 August. Here in Australia, anyway. Apparently in the Northern hemisphere it's on 1 January. I don't know why it can't be the same all over the world!

So, we celebrated my babies birthdays this afternoon when I got home from school. I made them 2 special horsey cakes with all their favorites. I included some oats and chaff, 2 large grated carrots, some chopped up apple and banana (Sparkle's favourite) and then added some molasses and honey to help bind it all together and as an extra sweet treat. Then I put them on 2 separate plates and even put candles on top. Mom, Dad, Nate and I all sang happy birthday and I blew out the candles for them.

Tara and Sparkle were so good. The candles didn't bother them at all. I think they were too interested in what was on the plate to be worried about candles. They certainly enjoyed their treat, that's for sure!

## Sunday 3 August

Something happened at pony club today that I was not expecting. I was doing rider class and I'd just finished telling my favorite instructor, Kylie, that I had won first place in the gymkhana a couple of weeks ago. And then Tara started to pig root. I've seen horses do this before, but I've never experienced it myself. It gave me a bit of a fright at first but I kept on riding. Then she did it again – and again – and again! I started to get scared and Kylie told me to be firm with her and use a gruff voice to tell her to stop. But she just kept doing it and I had to hop off. I didn't know what was wrong! All I did know was that she was really scaring me!

Kylie could see how upset I was and decided to hop on her herself. But Tara just kept pig rooting and wouldn't stop. She told me that Tara was probably in season and being a moody mare and that I shouldn't do the class. That was really upsetting because I just had to stand and watch. I didn't know why Tara was behaving like that!

One of the moms told me that if she is in season it would explain her behavior. She said that there is actually a vaccination that can be given to prevent this and suggested we speak to the vet. Mom and I didn't like the sound of that, but think we might try the herbal medicine that she said is also available for moody mares. I guess this is another reason why geldings are so popular!

After the class finished, one of the other girls, Jackie, who's a pretty experienced rider, hopped on Tara and took her for a ride. She did a few pig roots but Jackie was really firm with her, using her voice and some taps of her crop. This made Tara settle right down and behave. Jackie said that I'm going to have to learn to do the same thing if Tara keeps behaving like this and let her know that I'm the boss.

I went to my next class and when Tara tried it again, I was able to manage her a lot better. But then in the afternoon classes, she just kept pigrooting and I wasn't able to do much riding at all. Maybe she's just trying to be in control or maybe she's in season. Or, maybe it's a combination of both.

Mom rang Tracey tonight to tell her what had happened and she said that if Tara ever misbehaved with Josh, that he would just be firm with her and not put up with it. But she said that it didn't happen very much and wasn't really too much of a problem. It seems to be a lot worse when I'm riding her though! And I wonder why?

We want to get on top of this as soon as possible, so Mom and Dad have decided to arrange for a horse trainer to come to our house to work with her. She's instructed at pony club before and apparently is really good with problem horses.

But Tara can't possibly be a problem horse! I haven't had her very long and she's my dream pony!! I hope that the trainer can come soon though. I want my dream pony back!!!

*One of the instructors at pony club*

## Wednesday 6 August

I don't know what to do! I've just had the worst news and I'm actually freaking out right now!! I've spent most of the afternoon in my room. And I feel sick with worry.

The horse trainer came today. And I can't believe what she told us!!!

First of all we tacked Tara up and then Janice the trainer, checked out her saddle to make sure it was sitting correctly on her back. She didn't really find any problems there, so next she began to longe her. To begin with, Tara was cooperating, but then she suddenly started to pig root. And she wouldn't stop! She got so bad that she actually almost looked dangerous! I was really scared! But Janice was really firm with her and managed to calm her down so she could hop on. Within minutes though, she hopped off again. She said that she didn't want to risk riding her because she was being so hard to handle. I didn't really blame her! There was no way I was going to get on her while she was like that, that's for sure!

I asked Janice - Why is she suddenly behaving like this?

I just couldn't understand it. But it was her answer that shocked me even more than Tara's behavior!

"This horse is a nightmare! You need to get rid of her!"

That is what she told me. I could not believe what I was hearing! How could she say that about my dream pony? It just doesn't make sense! She's been absolutely perfect until now. There must be a reason why she's behaving this way.

Janice said that there's a possibility she's been drugged by her previous owners so they could sell her. She said that the calming effects can last a few months, then the new owners are stuck with the psycho horse that they've bought.

I just know that Tracey wouldn't do something like this! And Mom and Dad agree. There's no way that this could have happened to Tara. Tracey loves her and was genuinely upset to be selling her.

But Janice is adamant that we've bought a real problem horse in Tara. And says that she can try to work with her and get her to a stage where she can be sold.

When I got back to the house this afternoon, I just ran into my room and started to cry. And I've been here ever since. This can't be happening. Tara is my dream pony. We've been through so many problems with Sparkle, I just wanted a pony that I can enjoy and have fun on.

What am I going to do?

If we have to sell her, there's no way Mom and Dad will buy me another horse! I know them – they'll just say that's it! No more!! It's all too hard and maybe you're better off without a horse at all.

But what about Tara? What's going to happen to her? Janice even said that horses like her often end up at the doggers. That's where they take horses and kill them for dog meat.

I can't let this happen. There has to be more to it. Why would she suddenly start to behave like this? It just doesn't make any sense!

We can't just give up on her! We just can't!!!!

# PLEASE SAVE MY BABY!!!!

*Find out what happens next*

*in Book 3 of*

*Diary of a Horse Mad Girl…*

Thank you for reading my book.

If you enjoyed it, I would be very grateful if you would leave a review on Amazon.

Your support really does make a difference!

*Please Like our Diary of a Horse Mad Girl Facebook page*

*- A fabulous page for all horse loving girls...*

https://www.facebook.com/DiaryofaHorseMadGirl

..

Made in the USA
Middletown, DE
12 July 2020